PUFFIN BOOKS

Diz and the Big Fat Burglar

Other titles in the First Young Puffin series

BEAR'S BAD MOOD John Prater
BELLA AT THE BALLET Brian Ball
BLESSU Dick King-Smith
BUBBLEGUM BOTHER Wendy Smith
DAD, ME AND THE DINOSAURS Jenny Koralek
THE DAY THE SMELLS WENT WRONG Catherine Sefton
THE DAY WE BRIGHTENED UP THE SCHOOL Mick Gowar
DUMPLING Dick King-Smith
ERIC'S ELEPHANT GOES CAMPING John Gatehouse
ERIC'S ELEPHANT ON HOLIDAY John Gatehouse
FETCH THE SLIPPER Sheila Lavelle
GERALDINE GETS LUCKY Robert Leeson
GOODNIGHT, MONSTER Carolyn Dinan
HAPPY CHRISTMAS, RITA! Hilda Offen
HARRY'S AUNT Sheila Lavelle
HOP IT, DUGGY DOG! Brian Ball
THE INCREDIBLE SHRINKING HIPPO Stephanie Baudet
THE JEALOUS GIANT Kaye Umansky
NINA THE GOBBLEDEGOAT Penny Ives
PINK FOR POLAR BEAR Valerie Solís
THE POCKET ELEPHANT Catherine Sefton
THE QUEEN'S BIRTHDAY HAT Margaret Ryan
RAJ IN CHARGE Andrew and Diana Davies
RITA THE RESCUER Hilda Offen
RITA IN WONDERWORLD Hilda Offen
ROLL UP! ROLL UP! IT'S RITA Hilda Offen
THE ROMANTIC GIANT Kaye Umansky
SPACE DOG SHOCK Andrew and Paula Martyr
SOS FOR RITA Hilda Offen
THANK YOU DUGGY DOG Brian Ball and Lesley Smith
WHAT STELLA SAW Wendy Smith
WOOLLY JUMPERS Peta Blackwell

Diz and the Big Fat Burglar

Margaret Stuart Barry

Illustrated by

Paula Lawford

PUFFIN BOOKS

For Nick Bate

PUFFIN BOOKS

Published by the Penguin Group
Penguin Books Ltd, 80 Strand, London WC2R 0RL, England
Penguin Putnam Inc., 375 Hudson Street, New York, New York 10014, USA
Penguin Books Australia Ltd, 250 Camberwell Road, Camberwell, Victoria 3124, Australia
Penguin Books Canada Ltd, 10 Alcorn Avenue, Toronto, Ontario, Canada M4V 3B2
Penguin Books India (P) Ltd, 11 Community Centre, Panchsheel Park, New Delhi – 110 017, India
Penguin Books (NZ) Ltd, Cnr Rosedale and Airborne Roads, Albany, Auckland, New Zealand
Penguin Books (South Africa) (Pty) Ltd, 24 Sturdee Avenue, Rosebank 2196, South Africa

Penguin Books Ltd, Registered Offices: 80 Strand, London WC2R 0RL, England

www.penguin.com

First published by Hamish Hamilton Ltd 1987
Published in Puffin Books 1996
11 13 15 17 19 20 18 16 14 12

Printed and bound in China by Leo Paper Products Ltd

0–140–37531–7

Diz was a small girl aged six and a half. She lived with her dog, Digger, in a VERY messy house.

"Just look at my corner!" Digger growled. "I can't find my rubber bone."

The postman was cross too. He had to climb up a ladder and post the letters through the bedroom window.

"All right," Diz sighed. "I suppose we'd better tidy up."

Digger was pleased. He rushed around, wagging his tail and barking a song he knew about Spring cleaning.

Diz put on a bright pair of overalls, and found a fluffy feather duster.

Digger fetched a shovel and a sweeping brush.

They started to tidy Digger's corner first.

They found a cricket bat, a pink bear with one eye missing, a cracked teapot, a mouse, a broken doll, Digger's rubber bone and –

a BIG FAT BURGLAR who was fast asleep.

Diz and Digger tidied up the good things and threw away the broken ones. But they didn't know what to do with the burglar.

"We can't very well tidy HIM up," said Digger.

"And we can't very well throw him away," said Diz.

They sat down for a rest and a think, and stared at the burglar.

"Give him a dust," said Digger.

So Diz tickled him with her feather duster.

The burglar woke up, and sneezed very loudly.

"You're a BURGLAR!" Diz said.

The burglar looked down at his stripey jumper and sackful of stolen things.

"So I am!" he said, and fell asleep again.

Diz and Digger went to see Sergeant Scoop at the Police Station.

"We have a big fat burglar in our house. Please would you come and collect him at once," Diz said.

"Certainly," said Sergeant Scoop, who didn't believe Diz one little bit. "I'll come along when I've finished my dinner."

Sergeant Scoop went and told the Chief Inspector that there was a silly little kid, with a silly little dog, who had a dangerous criminal in their house.

"Gosh!" yawned the Chief Inspector.

When Diz and Digger got home, they found the burglar had been busy. He had finished tidying Digger's corner. He had done all the washing-up, and had made some delicious scones.

Diz and Digger felt guilty.

Just before bedtime, the burglar filled all the hot-water bottles and set the table for morning.

"I wonder why Sergeant Scoop hasn't come?" whispered Digger.

"Perhaps he has more important criminals to catch," said Diz, hopefully.

Next day, the burglar said,

"Oh gosh! I seem to have your clock in my sack. It must have dropped in by mistake."

And he put it back on the mantelpiece.

Then the burglar went out into the garden and dug it all over. He planted peas and beans, carrots and onions.

That evening he knitted a bright red cardigan for Diz, and a woolly hat with ear-flaps for Digger.

The more good things the big fat burglar did, the more Diz and Digger wished they hadn't reported him to Sergeant Scoop.

"Oh gosh!" said the burglar, "I've found your valuable pot. It must have fallen into my sack."

And he put it back on the table.

There was still no sign of Sergeant Scoop. He was playing Snap with the Chief Inspector. Sergeant Scoop was cheating.

Diz and Digger were pleased. They didn't want the big fat burglar to go to prison after all. They decided they should take him back to his own house where he would be safe.

"Get all your stuff together," Diz told him.

Digger wagged his tail at the thought of a walk.

The burglar led the way back to his house. It was next door to the Police Station.

Diz knocked on the door. "We've brought your husband back," she said.

"Oh, thanks," said Mrs Burglar, setting out three more silver cups.

"I think your husband should stop stealing," said Diz.

Mrs Burglar looked astonished, and so did all the little Burglar children.

"But he's always been a burglar!" she cried. "And a good one, too."

Then all the little Burglar children began to cry loudly.

"There's a terrible noise going on in the house next door, Sergeant Scoop," complained the Chief Inspector. "You'd better go and see what's happening. Perhaps they've got a burglar."

"Hullo, hullo, hullo," said Sergeant Scoop as he went into the big fat burglar's sitting-room. "Is everything all right?"

Sergeant Scoop didn't notice the silver football cups, or the twenty television sets, or the golden spoons, or the famous paintings on the walls, or the fifty electric toasters.

"Everything's fine," said the burglar.

Sergeant Scoop went back to the Police Station. "They are having a tea party, I think. That silly little girl and her silly little dog are there too."

"SNAP!" said the Chief Inspector, who had also been cheating.

Meanwhile, Diz had thought of a brilliant idea.

"My house is FULL of things," she said. "Anything you need, just come and ask me. Then you won't need to steal!"

So whenever the Burglar family wanted something, they asked Diz. And that way, the big fat burglar stayed out of prison, and Diz's house stayed nice and tidy – and so did Digger's corner!

Also available in First Young Puffin

BLESSU
Dick King-Smith

The tall, flowering elephant-grasses give Blessu hay-fever. 'BLESS YOU!' all the elephants cry whenever little Blessu sneezes, which is very often. Blessu grows slowly except for one part of him – his trunk – and his sneeze becomes the biggest, loudest sneeze in the world!

THE DAY THE SMELLS WENT WRONG
Catherine Sefton

It is just an ordinary day, but Jackie and Phil can't understand why nothing smells as it should. Toast smells like tar, fruit smells like fish, and their school dinners smell of perfume!

Together, Jackie and Phil discover the cause of the problem . . .

WHAT STELLA SAW
Wendy Smith

Stella's mum is a fortune-teller who always gets things wrong. But when football-mad Stella starts reading tea-leaves, she seems to be right every time! Or is she . . .